The Technic Companion

A first guide to the essentials of piano playing and musical interpretation by DENES AGAY and NANCY BACHUS.

Cover and interior illustrations by Janice Fried
Interior design and music engraving by Don Giller

Copyright © 1990 Yorktown Music Press, Inc.

Order No. YK 20600
US International Standard Book Number: 0.8256.8081.6
UK International Standard Book Number: 0.7119.1913.5

Exclusive Distributors:
Music Sales Corporation
225 Park Avenue South, New York, NY 10003 USA
Music Sales Limited
8/9 Frith Street, London W1V 5TZ England
Music Sales Pty. Limited
120 Rothschild Street, Rosebery, Sydney, NSW 2018, Australia

Printed in the United States of America by
Vicks Lithograph and Printing Corporation

Yorktown Music Press, Inc.
New York/London/Sydney

Table of Contents

How to Use This Book

The Technic Companion is designed to be used in conjunction with any standard piano primer. It provides technical guidance from the very first lesson by outlining and developing the basic concepts and skills that will serve the student throughout his or her pianistic career, be it for personal pleasure or professional vocation. On the guiding discipline that piano playing uses different movements for different sounds and effects, we have laid the groundwork for playing the piano with not just the fingers but the entire body. Playing begins with the third finger, expanding soon to the second, third and fourth. Finally, leaping octaves are used to promote ease of playing throughout the keyboard. Special attention is given to the first and fifth fingers (frequent troublemakers) to complete five-finger patterns, double notes and triads, with suggestions on how to practice them. All concepts and patterns are applied in attractive pieces especially written to not only advance technical ease and coordination but also to please.

To further achieve technical agility and refinement, a primary emphasis of *The Technic Companion* is to develop a variety of touches (legato, staccato), phrasing patterns (two-note slurs, larger groupings) and to establish independence of hands. Focus on only one specific task in each exercise or piece; this will permit practice and fluency before combining it with another technic formula in the other hand. (How can we expect a student to play legato in one hand and staccato in the other when he or she can play neither well?)

The Technic Companion is written not only for the *beginner* who is just learning the basics and establishing sound playing habits but also for the *more advanced student* who may be lacking in real technical control and refinement and who can benefit greatly by reviewing and perfecting the technical disciplines outlined in this text. We encourage a weekly assignment of a variety of patterns and touches to be used as a "warm-up" at the beginning of the student's practice and heard at the beginning of each lesson. This establishes good habits, patterns and touches "in the hand."

It is not necessary to teach The Technic Companion *in order*. It is a resource to aid the teacher and student. The five-finger patterns, triads, and touches, for example, could be introduced in correlation with their current repertoire as reinforcement or as a different approach to a problem.

Since it is impossible to separate technic and interpretation, students are encouraged to produce different tone qualities, touches, and dynamics through technical suggestions, and focus on listening and appealing to their imaginations. It is emphasized throughout that playing the piano is not only physical function involving muscles and joints but also a mental/emotional process engaging the ear and the mind. As Robert Schumann once said, to be a good pianist, "you must have music not only in your fingers but also in your head and in your heart."

The Keyboard

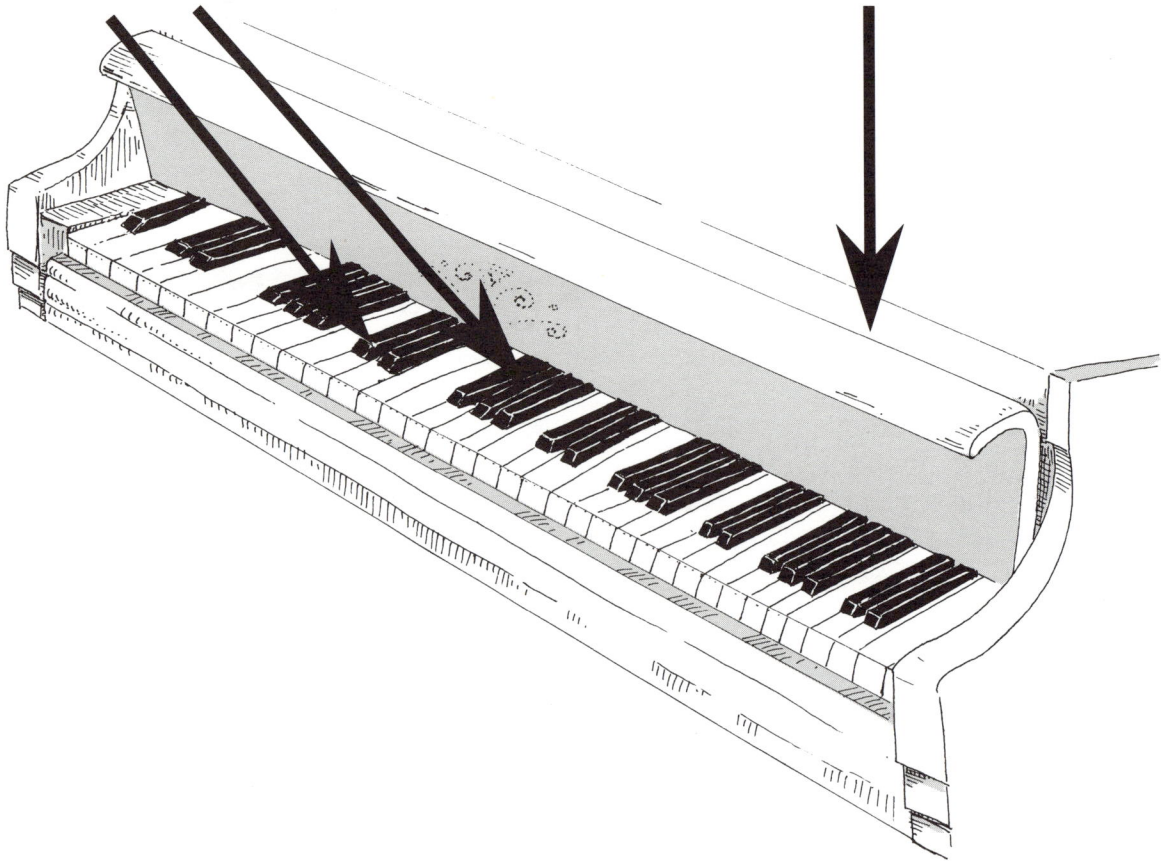

Finger Numbers

The thumb is the first finger of each hand.

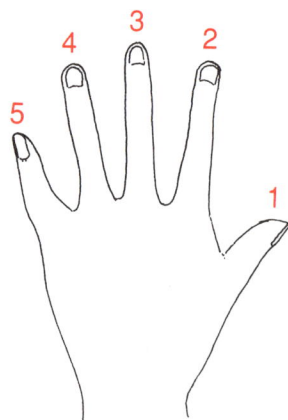

Left Hand

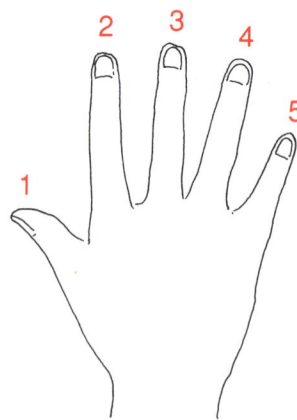

Right Hand

The Grand Staff

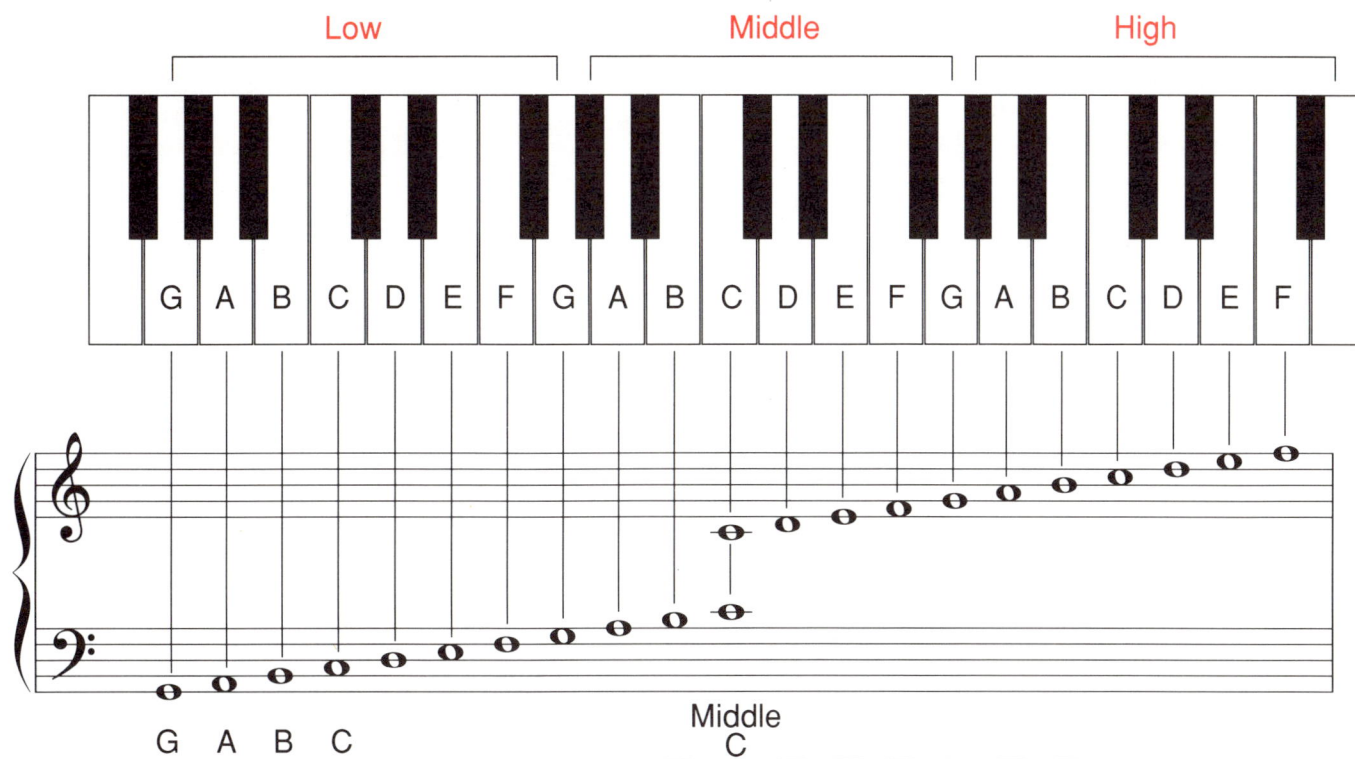

Low   Middle   High

G A B C D E F G A B C D E F G A B C D E F

G A B C   Middle C

Note Values

𝅝	**Whole-Note:** 4-count note
𝅗𝅥.	**Dotted Half-Note:** 3-count note
𝅗𝅥	**Half-Note:** 2-count note
𝅘𝅥	**Quarter-Note:** 1-count note
𝅘𝅥𝅮𝅘𝅥𝅮	**Two Eighth-Notes (equal the time value of one quarter-note):** 1-count note

How to Sit at the Piano

Observe:

- Back (spine) straight with just a hint of leaning slightly forward
- Shoulders relaxed
- Upper arms hanging loosely from the shoulders
- Forearms raised to the level of the keyboard (adjust bench if necessary)
- Feet firmly on the floor (Use footstool or box if feet do not reach.)
- Weight of the body is centered in hips and lower back.

Finding Your Natural Hand Position

1. Let your arms and hands hang loosely at your sides. Notice the "natural curve" of the relaxed hand. (This is the perfect hand position.)

2. Bring your hands up to the keyboard, bending at the elbows (see illustration on next page). Keep the natural curve of the hand.

3. Open or spread apart the palm of the hand (from knuckle of the fifth finger to the curved "nail joint" of the thumb).

4. Shake your hands loosely from the wrist, keeping the palm open and in its "natural curve."

Our Piano-Playing Machine

When playing the piano, **our entire body—from feet to fingertips—works together as a unit,** a wonderful **"playing machine."** Each part of this machine has its own special job, while all of its parts work together.

Our **joints** act as **"hinges,"** allowing us to move in many ways. **Sitting firmly** on the bench (with a straight back), you can **move forward and backward** with the hinge at your hips. (Your body leans slightly forward toward the keyboard when you play the piano.)

The other **main joints** used in piano playing are at the **shoulders, elbows**, **wrists**, and **knuckles**.

All these joints must feel "loose" when playing the piano.

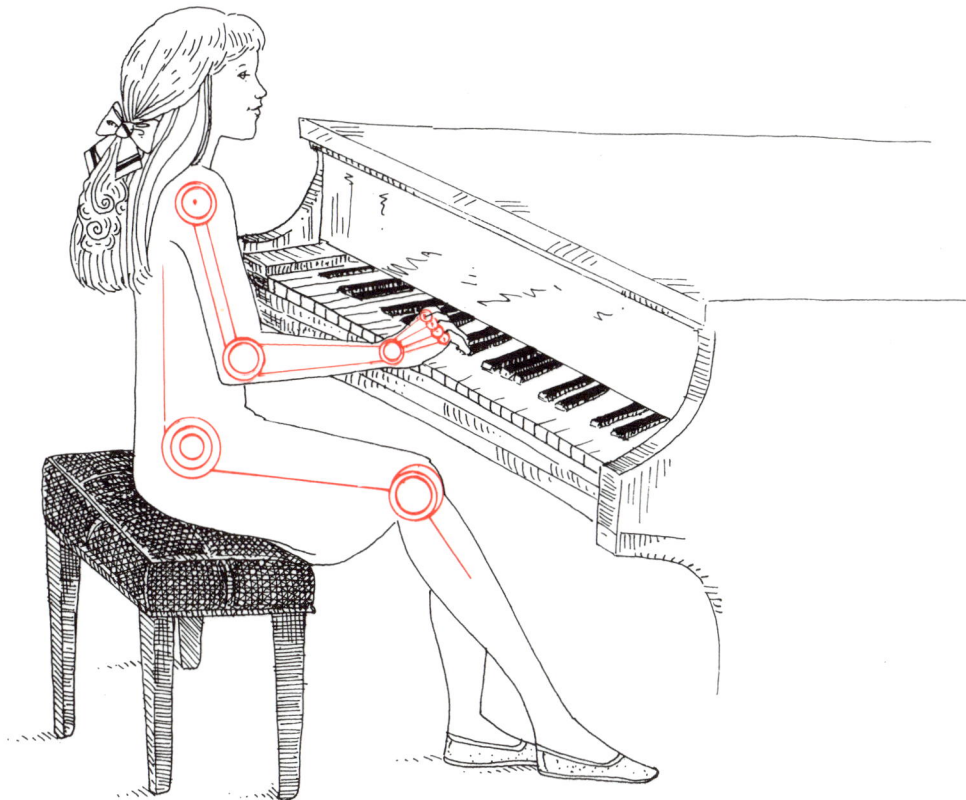

Exercises to Loosen Piano-Playing Joints

- **Shoulder Joint:** Let arms hang loosely at sides. Bend arms at the elbows. Move the upper arm backwards and forwards (toward and away from the keyboard) from the shoulder joint.

- **Elbow Joint:** With arms still bent at the elbow, move the forearm up and down (toward and away the knee) from the elbow joint.

- **Wrist Joint:** Using a "knocking" motion on the fallboard, move the hand up and down from the wrist joint.

- **Knuckle Joints:** Using a "drumming" motion with the fingers on the fallboard, move the fingers up and down from the knuckle joints.

Moving at the Joints in Rhythm

The teacher plays and sings "Let's Bend Our Arms" while the student moves (in ♩ or ♪ rhythm) at **shoulder joints**, **elbow joints, wrist joints**, and **knuckle joints**—moving exactly as in the previous exercise. The words and the numbers in the music tell you where to change movements.

Let's Bend Our Arms

Walking tempo

1. Move from shoulder joints.

Let's bend our arms at the el - bows, From the shoul - ders move your arms to and

2. Move from elbow joints.

fro. Now drum on your leg, Please don't make me beg. Just drum, drum, drum, let's

3. Move from the wrist joints.

go! On the fall - board knock with one fist, Then knock with the oth - er one
(ta - ble) *

4. Move from knuckle joints.

too. Now fin - ger - tips knock with the rhy - thm of a clock, not too hard or they'll get blue!

8   * Knock on a table if your teacher is playing the only piano.

"Falling" on Black Keys with Loose Fist

Exercise for "falling" in lap, with hands together:

1. Raise forearms (and hands), moving at the elbows.
2. Hold there a few seconds.
3. Release and let hand "fall" limply into your lap.

Exercise for "falling" on the keyboard, with left hand and then right hand:

1. Make a loose fist.
2. "Fall" (from the elbows) on any group of two black keys.
3. Then "fall" on any group of three black keys

Chinese Clock*

R.H. "falls" on three black keys

L.H. "falls" on two black keys

Ching, Chong, Ching, Chang, Chi-nese clocks you know don't chime, When they give the time. They sing Or-i-en-tal rhyme, in a per-fect time.

Bells Are Ringing

L.H. "falls" on three black keys

R.H. "falls" on three black keys

Notice the different "tone colors" as you change octaves of the keyboard.

Can you make the bells sound different (louder or softer) by falling from different heights?

Bells are ring-ing, ting-a-ling, Bells are ring-ing, ding, dong, ding.

* Pieces from here until page 19 should be taught primarily by rote (imitation).

Playing with Fingers 3 and 2

Very seldom are we asked to play with our fists on the keyboard. Most of the time our **fingertips** or **finger "nail joints" control the keys**. The way we play or put down the key with our fingertips will affect the **amount of sound** (softness, loudness), and the **quality of the sound** (rich, full, thin, harsh, and so on).

A beautiful tone is created when the finger "falls" and "settles into" the key, rather than "hitting" or "slapping" it.

With left hand and then right hand (third finger):

1. "Fall" (forearm action from the elbow) and "settle" into any key, black or white.

2. Keep a firm nail joint (not collapsed).

Two Black Keys

A. Play with two hands, alternating third fingers.

Two black keys,   Two black keys,   We can play on   two black keys.

B. Play with two hands, alternating two-note groups an octave apart. First play it with third fingers only, then with fingers 2-3-2 in the right hand and 3-2-3 in the left hand.

Two black keys,   Two black keys,   Lis - ten to   Two black keys.

Teacher duet part for A and B:

C. Two black keys played simultaneously in one hand. The two hands alternate, playing the two-note groups by octave jumps.

London Bridge

Two hands (third fingers) play together

Right hand, third finger on **D** (below middle C)

Left hand, third finger on **G** (below the D)

Remember:

1. "Fall" and "sink" into the key.
2. Feel the two keys go down exactly together.
3. Keep the fingers and hand in their natural curve; nail joints firm.

Also play "London Bridge" with second fingers.

Piano-Forte

The complete name for the piano is *pianoforte* from these Italian terms:
Piano (marked *p*), meaning soft   *Forte* (marked *f*) meaning loud

You can play the piano both softly and loudly. Composers use these terms (known as **dynamics**) to show the performer the amounts of sound they want in their music.

Increase in sound is marked by *Crescendo* (*cresc.*) – gradually louder:

Decrease in sound is marked by *Diminuendo* (*dim.*) – gradually softer:

One way to play different dynamics on the piano is by "falling" from different heights onto the key.

EXERCISE with separate hands, then with both hands:

1. Drop with the third finger several times, on any key.

2. Produce a soft tone and make it increasingly louder (*crescendo* from *p* to *f*). "Fall" from different heights, keeping the wrist "loose and bouncy."

3. Beginning higher above the key, then getting lower and lower, produce increasingly softer sounds (*diminuendo* from *f* to *p*). (It may be helpful to "fall" in your lap before trying it on the keyboard.)

Pass in Review

Student plays with alternating hands: **Right hand, third** finger on **F** below middle C
                                              Left hand, third finger on **F** one octave lower

Start *p* (close to the keys) as the parade approaches from a distance. Increase the sound as it comes nearer and nearer. Reach *f* (falling from a greater height) as the parade passes in front of you. Then decrease the sound gradually (*diminuendo*) and fade out as the parade leaves.

Playing with the Three Middle Fingers

First, find your natural hand position. (See page 6.)

Three Black Keys

Play the three-black-key groups an octave apart, with the three middle fingers in each hand. (Start on G♭.)

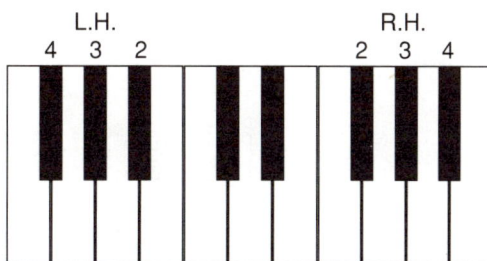

R.H. Three black keys, | Three black keys, | Lis - ten to | three black keys.

Up and Down (on Three White Keys)

Starting with two hands an octave apart on G, play first with the right hand and then with the left hand; then, if possible, play together.

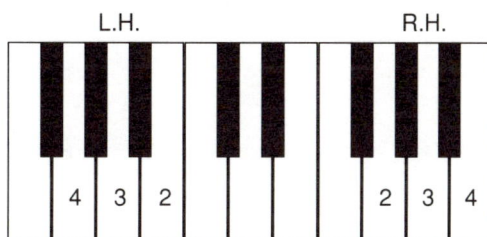

We go up, | We go down, | We go up and | down.

Mountain Climb

Three-note groups, jumping by octaves with alternating hands

Get the **same beautiful tone quality** with all three fingers (2-3-4).

- Make the first four measures sound like **one long line** to the top note.
- Make the last four measures sound like **one long line** to the bottom note.

Climb-ing up   moun-tains we're   climb-ing up   high.   Com-ing down   to the ground   and say good - bye.

13

Producing the Same Tone Quality

Rolling

After falling with the third finger on the first note, **transfer that pleasing, rich tone** to the neighboring keys.

- First, play the right hand beginning on the C above middle C
- Next, play the left hand beginning on middle C.
- Then play them together, if possible.

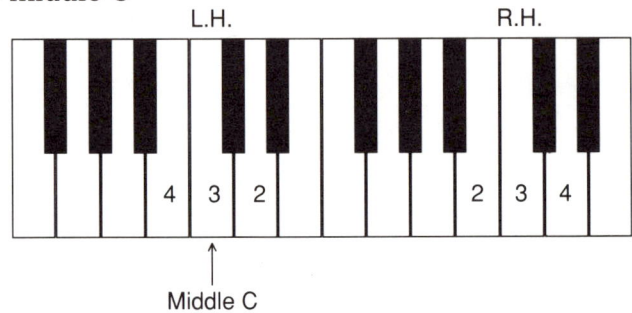

Merry-Go-Round

Play hands separately and then together.

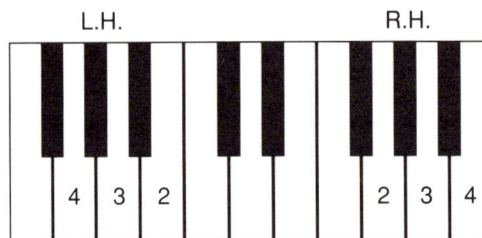

14

Jumping Octaves

L.H.: "Falls" and "sinks" into the key.
Nail joint is firm; wrist is level with forearm, yet loose and bouncy.

R.H.: "Falls" and then bounces off the key, moving in an arc
(half circle) to land on the next octave.

Hot Cross Buns (with Brass Band)

I

Student

Hot cross buns, Hot cross buns, One a pen-ny, Two a pen-ny, Hot cross buns.

Teacher

II

Student

Hot cross buns, Hot cross buns, One a pen-ny, Two a pen-ny, Hot cross buns.

Teacher

Kangaroos

Jumping two octaves in one hand

Jump - ing up,   Jump - ing down,   Jump - ing high,   like   a   clown.

Create moods when you play the piano.

Make the notes _mean_ something by creating feelings for you and your listeners.

You create moods by:

1. What you are thinking and feeling about the music as you play.

2. How you use your hands and fingers on the keys to create the mood you are feeling.

The composer gives us clues to the moods and feeling he intended in his music.

Usually these clues are:

the **Title**, the **Tempo**, and the **Dynamics** of the piece.

What are the moods of "Merry-Go-Round" and "Hot Cross Buns" (on pages 14 and 15)? How do they differ from "Cradle Song" ?

Cradle Song

Keep the same mood and same tone quality throughout the piece.

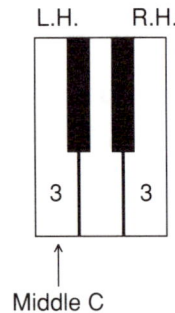

L.H.   R.H.

Middle C

E above middle C

R.H.

Rock - ing,   Rock - ing,   ba - by sleep to - night.   Rock - ing,   Rock - ing,   Dream 'till morn - ing   light.

L.H.

Middle C

Teacher

_p_

Fingers 1 and 5 Join the Middle fingers

Preparatory Exercise

1. Hold your hand in the air (upper arm hanging loosely; elbow bent; wrist relaxed and level with forearm; hand/palm open and in its natural curve).

2. Wiggle fingers 1 and 5 (fingers 2-3-4 remain quiet).

3. Put your two hands (with fingers in their natural curve) on the fallboard, table, or your legs.

4. Slightly extend fingers 1 and 5 outward (wider), keeping them curved.

5. "Walk" your hand forward and backward with fingers 1 and 5.

Walking Fingers

Teacher plays and sings while student "walks" fingers 1 and 5 on top of the piano or table. (When repeating song, student "walks" and joins singing.) Student may also play an ostinato to accompany teacher.

Student (ostinato)

L.H.   5   1

1   5

R.H.

Slow walking tempo

Just | look my fin-gers can | walk!　Per - | haps they can e - ven | talk!　They

al-most look a-live, both | "one" and "five," so come | on, don't balk, let's | walk!

Pieces for Fingers 1 and 5

Practice Suggestions

1. "Walk" fingers 1 and 5 (with arm quiet and fingers curved.)

2. When playing 1 and 5 together, the two fingers must touch the keys exactly together!

3. Play hands separately and then together, if possible.

Brass Band

mf Trom-bones play - ing | not too low. | Trum-pets fan - fare, | There they go!

Tu - bas join in | way down low. | Brass band warms up | for the | show!

Positioning Finger 5 (hands separately, at first)

1. Drop: **Right hand, third** finger on **E** above middle C or an octave higher.
   Left hand, third finger on **E** below middle C. Hold key down (knuckle joints firm but relaxed).

2. Without moving or changing position of finger 3, play finger 5 lightly several times, moving at the knuckle. (Hand and forearm are quiet.)

3. Make a richer tone by letting finger 5 "sink deeply into the key."

Positioning Finger 1 (the thumb)

Play hands separately, then together, if possible.

1. Drop: **Left hand, third** finger on the **E** below middle C.
   Right hand, third finger on the **E** two octaves higher.

2. Without moving or changing position of finger 3, play thumb lightly several times. (Hand and forearm remain quiet.) Thumb is played on side of fingertip near the nail, making a U-shape (not a V-shape) between fingers 1 and 2.

3. Produce a richer tone by letting the thumb sink more deeply into the key.

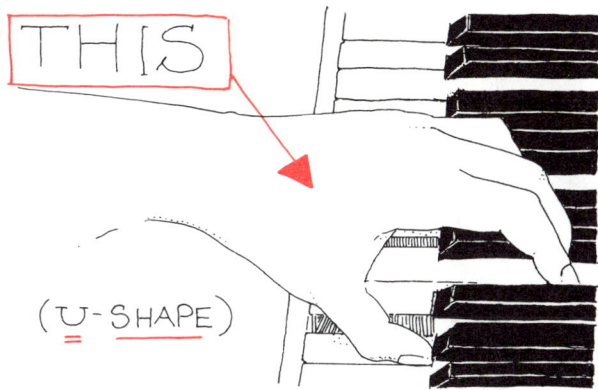

Jack and Jill

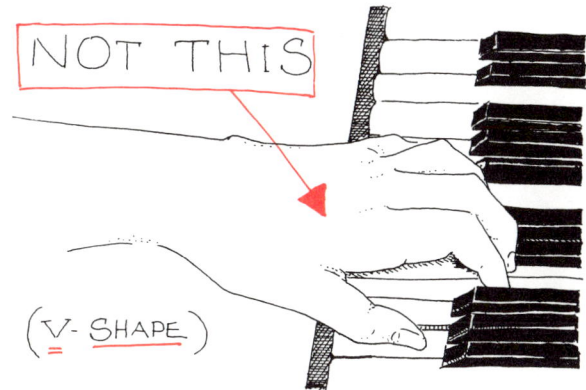

Skat - ing now are Jack - ie and Jill. Jack fell down, just like on the hill!

Complete Five-Finger Patterns

I. All Fingers on White Keys

- Fingers move at the knuckle joints, while hand and arm are quiet.
- Play all notes with firm fingertips at all speeds.
- *Listen* to produce even tones at all speeds.
- When speed increases, finger movements are smaller, shorter than at a slower pace. (At faster tempos fingers are "running," instead of "marching.")

♩ = 60-80

1 C Major

Count: 1 2 3 4   1 2 3 4   1 2 3 4   1 & 2 & 3 & 4 &   1 2 3 4

2 G Major

Also play L.H. one octave lower.

3 D Minor

4 A Minor

20

Pieces Using White-Key Finger Patterns

Remember: Hand in its natural curve—nail joints firm.

Warm-Up

See how high we go, Play-ing in a row. Let's go skip-ping now, I will show you how.

Before playing each piece, **play** its **five-finger pattern** (page 20) hands separately first, then together.

What a Day

What a day! What a day! All five fin-gers are at play!

G Major

Working Fingers

Work-ing fin-gers one by one, Play-ing all to-geth-er can be fun!

8va Play L.H. one octave lower.

A Minor

Skipping

Skip-ping high, Skip-ping low, Care-ful not to stub your toe.

Eighth-Note Bagatelles

D Minor

(Also play in A minor.)

One and two three four, one and two three four, one and two, three and four, one, two, three, four.

p   *f*   *D.C.*

G Major

8va - - - - - - - - - - - -

One two and three, one two and three, one two and three and one two and three.

mf   *D.C.*

8va - - - - - - - - - - - -
Play L.H. one octave lower.

Review of Dynamics

You have been playing *forte* with full, rich tone, and *piano* more softly. You have also been **increasing**,

(*crescendo, cresc.*, ⟨⟩) and **decreasing** (*decrescendo, diminuendo, dim.*, ⟩⟨) the sound.

- Notice that playing *forte* feels different in your fingers than playing *piano*.
- Always **think the sound you want** (the dynamics and the mood) **before playing**.

Other Dynamic Markings

pp	p	mp	mf	f	ff
Pianissimo	*Piano*	*Mezzo-Piano*	*Mezzo-Forte*	*Forte*	*Fortissimo*

II. Third Finger on Black Key

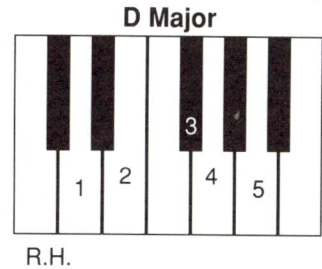

D Major

R.H.

Third on Black

"Third" on black, "third" on black, up we go and then turn back.

Play complete five-finger patterns in the following positions.

5 D Major

6 A Major

Continue as D pattern.

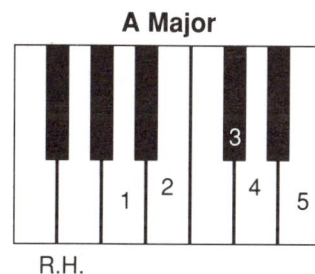

A Major

R.H.

7 C Minor

Continue as D pattern.

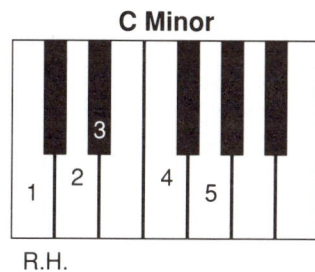

C Minor

R.H.

8 G Minor

Continue as D pattern.

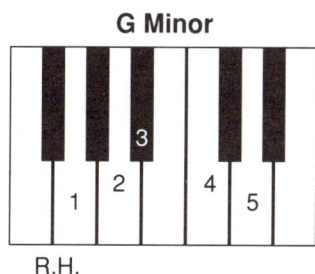

G Minor

R.H.

23

Pieces Using Third-on-Black-Key Patterns

No-No-No

Note repetition with the same finger

- Play the repeated notes with matching tone quality and length.
- Practice with separate hands and then together.

D Major

No, No, No, No, No, No, We don't mind the rain and snow,

We don't fret if we get wet, so grab your coat, let's go, go, go!

Swinging

Blowing Wind

A Major

- Play the following three pieces, and decide their mood (tempo, dynamics).
- Write in the tempo marks and dynamic signs; then play the pieces as marked.

G Minor

Sad

I feel so bad. I feel so sad. But play-ing well Makes me feel glad!

G Major

Glad

I know how to play it, play it, play it! I know how to play it, yes, I do!

I'm so glad to say it, I can play it. I know how to play it. Yes, I do!

R.H.-C Minor

L.H.-C Major

Blue Echo

III. More Five-Finger Patterns With One Black Key

(F Major and E Minor)

Left hand, second finger on B♭   **Right hand, fourth** finger on B♭

F Major Position

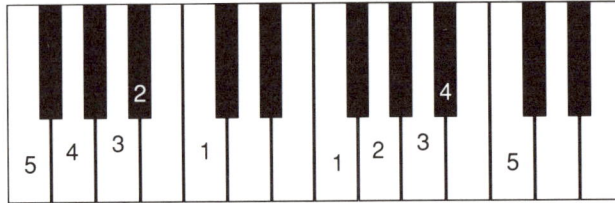

9 F Major

Gentle Request

Gently flowing
(Watch the key signature)

Playful Request

Begin your "request" carefully. When more confident, play somewhat faster.

Brisk walking tempo

Left hand, fourth finger on **F♯**   **Right hand, second** finger on **F♯**

E Minor Position

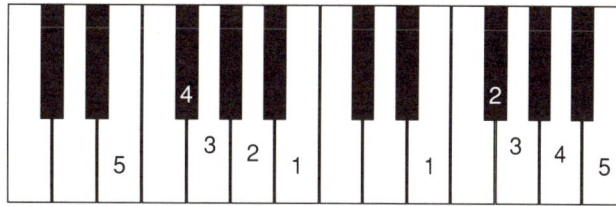

10 **E Minor**

Russian Song

Rather slow

p

Russian Dance

Lively

f

mf   *p*   *f*

27

IV. Five-Finger Patterns with Two Black Keys

(E Major and F Minor)

Left Hand **fourth** finger on F♯ **third** finger on G♯ **Right Hand** **second** finger on F♯ **third** finger on G♯

E Major Position

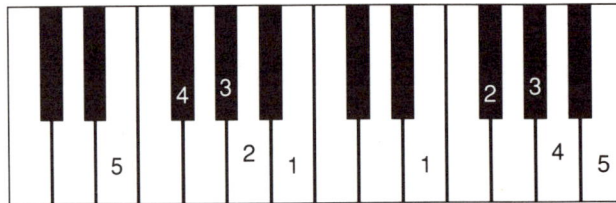

11 E Major

Leisurely Bike Ride

Moderato

Bike Race

Lively

Left Hand **third** finger on **A♭**
second finger on **B♭**

Right Hand **third** finger on **A♭**
fourth finger on **B♭**

F Minor Position

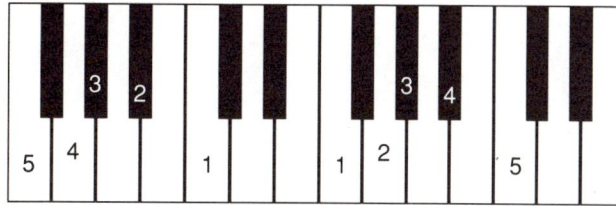

12 F Minor

Spinning

Moderate-to-lively

p

crescendo

mf

crescendo

p

mf

f

decrescendo

p

29

Touch

In piano playing, *touch* is the way the finger makes the key go down to produce a tone. The various ways a key is struck will affect:

- the **volume** of the tone (loud, soft, medium, etc.)
- the **length** of the tone (long, short, etc.), and
- the **quality** of the tone ("singing," "bouncy," rough, sweet, etc.)

Touch also means the way two or more successive notes are connected or separated. (This is the most commonly used meaning.) In this sense, the **two main piano touches** are:

legato or **connected**, and
staccato or **detached**.

Legato Touch

Legato, an Italian word, means "bound together." Its sign is a curved line (slur) placed over or under two or more notes:

Notes "bound together" by a slur are to played *legato*, in a smooth, connected manner, without any break or gap between the notes.

To connect notes with legato touch:

- Move fingers from the knuckles
- Allow a depressed key to rise only when the next key is already fully depressed by another finger.
- *Listen* carefully that the sound continues without break from note to note.

Practice all fingering combinations.

The arrow indicates where the finger that just played the preceding note is lifted.

Legato Tune
Shifting five-finger patterns

Moderato

Let's go step by | step and play a | tune. | We can play it | morn-ing, night, and | noon.

Just a sim-ple, | sing-a-ble re- | frain. | Five notes up and | five notes down a- | gain.

G Minor

Sailing at Sunset

Sail-ing at | sun-set when | calm is the | sea, Red | clouds and blue | wa-ters are | love-ly to | see.

31

Staccato Touch

Staccato is the Italian word for "detached," making a *staccato* touch the opposite of a *legato* touch. While *legato* touch creates a smooth, sustained sound, *staccato* touch produces short, crisp, detached tones. *Staccato* (*stacc.*) is marked by a small dot over or under the note head:

Playing staccato involves two combined motions in quick succession:

1. A quick, firm fingertip "attack" depressing the key.
2. Swift, instant "rebound" from the key. After striking the key, the finger (with the aid of the hand and wrist) bounces back instantly and returns to its raised position.

These two motions ("attack" and "rebound") *involve both finger action and wrist action.* We distinguish between **wrist staccato** and **finger staccato**, depending on which is more pronounced.

Jumping Jack
Wrist staccato

- "Knock" with a loose fist on the fallboard or on any black key group.
- Using the same "knocking" motion from the wrist, play "Jumping Jack," all with the third finger.
- Listen for a "bouncy" sound on each note.

Jump-ing, jump-ing up and down. Jump-ing, jump-ing like a clown.

Hop! Skip! Jump! Hop! Skip! Jump!

Peter, Peter, Pumpkin Eater

Wrist staccato

- Play with "knocking" motion from the wrist, all on third finger.
- Use alternating hands. (Left hand plays G♭ throughout the piece.)
- In measures 2, 4, and 6, right hand crosses over left hand.

(All on black keys.)

Pe - ter, Pe - ter, pump-kin eat - er, Had a wife and could - n't keep her,

Put her in a pump-kin shell, and there he kept her ve - ry well!

D Minor

Little Miss Butterfly

Finger staccato

- Play with very pointed, firm fingertips for crisp, dainty tone quality.
- On each note, the fingers (except the thumb) "pull back" off the key towards the palm of the hand, like "flicking dust" off the key.
- Play at various speeds (between *andante* and *allegretto*).
- The finger strokes will be shorter at a faster tempo .

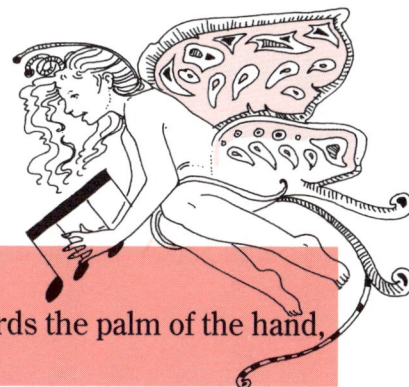

Graceful moderato

Sidney Jones

Hear the Clock
Combined wrist and finger staccato

- On longer staccato notes (♩ ♩) you use bigger motions, such as falling from the elbow, allowing the wrist to have flexibility.
- On faster notes when there is less time (♫), the hand moves at the wrist in a smaller "knocking" motion. There is also more finger action at faster speeds.

Moderato

Hear the clock,   Hear the clock,   Tick-Tock, Tick-Tock   Tick-Tock, Tick-Tock

Big clock, Lit-tle clock   Big clock, Lit-tle clock   Ding   Dong   Cuck-oo   Cuck-oo

F Major

Woodpecker Serenade
Combined wrist and finger staccato

On the eighth-note rhythms ( ), you may knock on the wood of the piano , clap your hands, or make other appropriate sounds (in correct rhythm!).

My wood-peck-er   ser-e-nade,   Hear it on the   hit-pa-rade.

Ev-'ry-bod-y   tap-tap-tap,   clap-clap-clap,   rap-rap-rap.

The Language of Music

Music is a language—with tones instead of words.

In *language*,	words are grouped into *sentences* and other smaller units to express a thought and to give meaning.
In *music*,	tones are grouped into various melody units called *phrases* to form a larger musical structure, such as a complete "sentence" or "piece."
In *written language*,	there are commas, periods, and other *punctuation marks* to show and separate word groups, making their meaning clearer.
In *written music*,	the *slur* is the clearest mark to indicate which notes belong together and which notes should be separated from other melody units.

Because of this, a secure technic for the correct interpretation of slurs is very important; it gives music its shape and meaning.

Two-Note Slurs

Here are two examples of two notes of different pitches connected by a slur:

A two-note slur has two notes played legato, with a graceful "release" on the second note. (See Step 4 below.)

Playing a Two-Note Slur

1. Poise your hand above the keys to be played. (Put hand in its natural playing position, elbow bent with the wrist somewhat higher.)
2. "Fall" into the first key.by dropping the wrist (to level with the forearm and hand) and letting the weight of the hand and arm "sink" into the key as the finger depresses it. (Feel the firm fingertip.)
3. After the first key is fully depressed, play the second note with legato touch.
4. Continue the motion on the the second note; hand and arm follow through in a forward direction,"floating" towards the fallboard as the wrist rises.
5. After releasing the second key, the hand will be in the air again (above the keyboard), ready for the next gesture (repeating steps 2, and 3, and 4).

Remember: The two notes of the slur do not have the same tone-quality. The **first note** getting the weight of the hand and arm is usually **fuller-sounding**, more sonorous than the second.

D Minor

Flying

- First, play with fingers 2-3 (right hand) and 3-2 (left hand) only.
- Then play with fingering as marked.

Fly - ing | in the | wild blue | yon - der,

How high | am I, | I just | won - der.

Oh, Me, Oh, My!

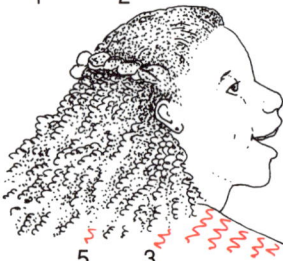
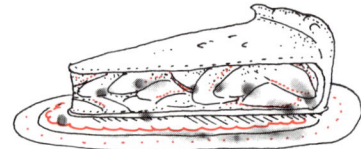

Oh, me, | Oh, my, | Now I'll | say good - bye,

To this | great big | piece of | ap - ple | pie!

G Major

Crossing Puddles

Three-or-More-Note Slurs

The technic of playing three-note, four-note, or five-note slurs is essentially the same as playing two-note slurs. They all require the same graceful, coordinated gesture of the finger, hand, wrist, and arm.

1. Drop wrist (to level with forearm/hand) into the first note and let the weight sink into the finger as it depresses the key.

2. Play the subsequent notes with legato touch, allowing the wrist to raise gradually.

3. The arm and hand follow through in a forward direction (in simultaneous movement with the wrist) for a graceful release on the last note of the slur.

The above three-part gesture should be the same whether the slur combines two, three, or five notes:

What Do You Like to Eat?

Laura's Dancing

Gracefully

Grandma's Presents

Four-note slur

Comfortably

Rock - ing chairs are | made for sit - ting, | Just for grand - mas | who like knit - ting,

Jack - ets, and socks, | and mit - tens, too. | Lov - ing pres - ents | for me and you.

Singing Proverb

Moderato

Ear - ly to bed, | Ear - ly to rise,

Makes a man health - y, | Wealth - y and wise.

More About "Releases"

The size of the gesture (motion) that releases the key on the last note of the slur will not always be the same. It can be a large or small motion. If there is a longer note or rest at the end of the slur, there is time for a big release movement. When the music flows at an uninterrupted, lively pace, the release motion must be smaller, sometimes barely noticeable.

The small motion of release will be marked with a ,.

The larger release gesture will be marked with a ↑.

"Time" the size of your release movement to the rhythm and tempo of the music.

Larger Legato Groupings

The secret of fluency, speed, and effective shaping of melodies lies in grouping several notes with one large gesture of hand, wrist, and arm. This is what you've been doing when playing slurs connecting two to five or six notes.

When the slur is a long one, extending over several measures and many notes, play with an even legato, maintaining the same tone quality from note to note. *There will be a release motion only on the last note of the slur.* (Review pages 30 and 31.)

First play the left hand. Then play the right hand two octaves higher. Finally, play both hands together.

Now play "Legato Tune" (page 31) again, with an even, beautiful **legato** touch and a graceful release on all dotted half notes (𝅗𝅥.).

Slurred legato notes divided between the hands (crossover)

- Keep your upper arm hanging limply from the shoulder. (Elbow is bent.)
- Cross over by moving mainly from the elbow in an arc-shaped leap.
- Wrists are loose and bouncy. Nail joints are firm.

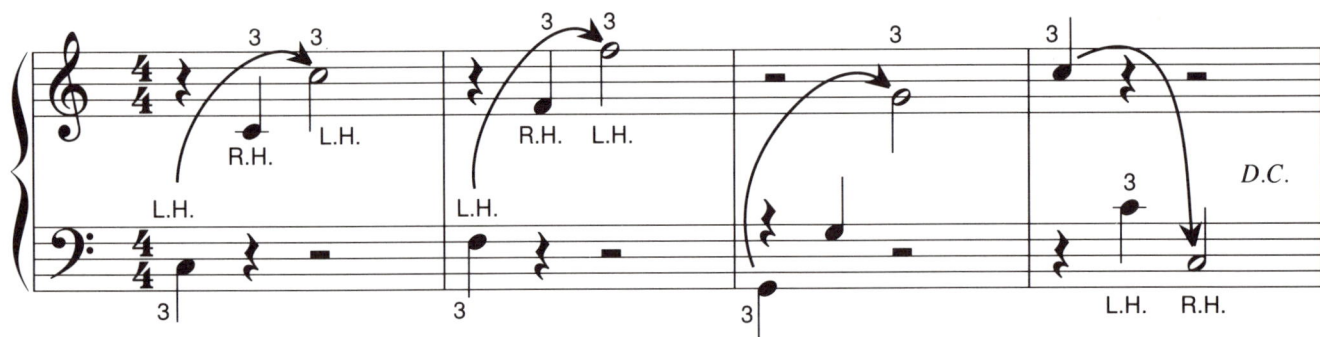

The Glider

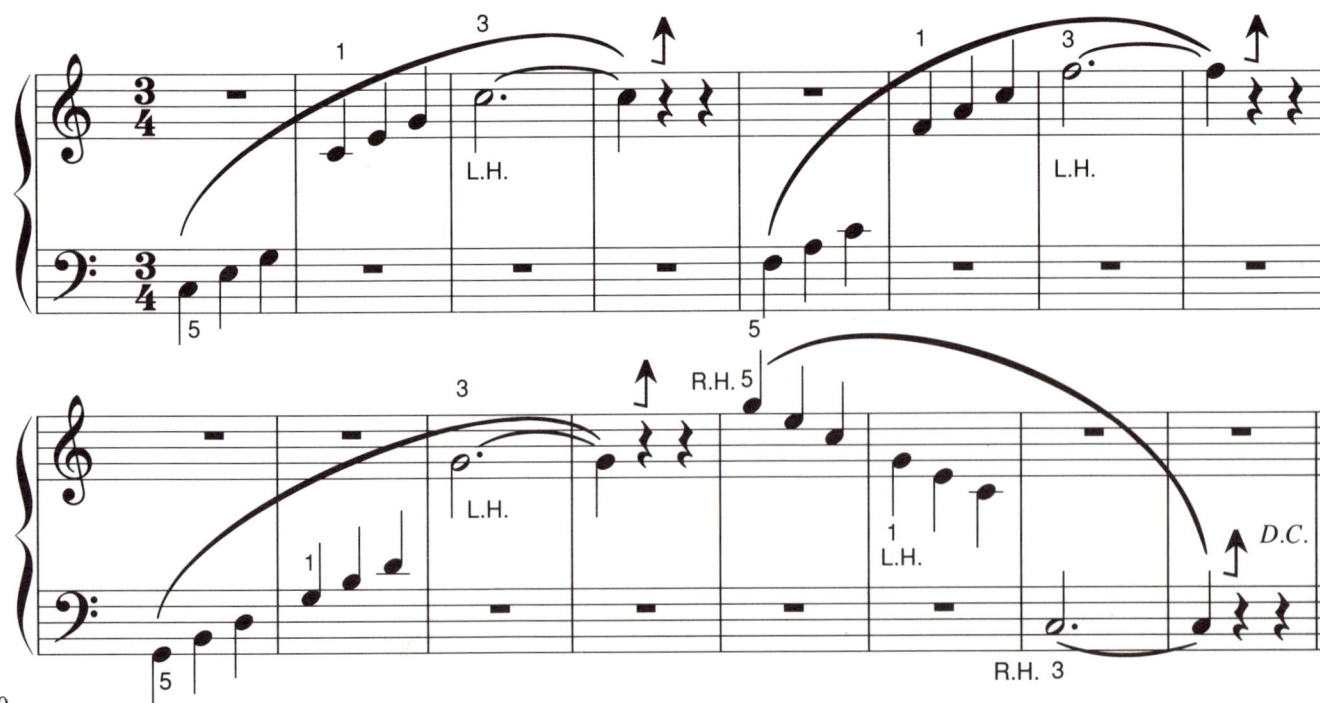

Combining Legato and Staccato Touches
Variations on "Legato Tune"*
With some hidden thoughts

p finger staccato
f wrist staccato

(Can I do this?)

mf (Let's try, anyway...)

f (Sure I can do it...and it's fun!)

p (What do you think?) *f* (Great job!)

D Major

> = Accent Mark
(Maintain a beautiful tone quality)

Round Dance

mf

* "Legato Tune" can be found on page 30.

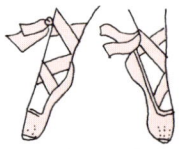

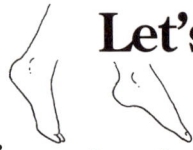

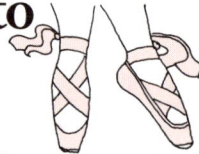

Let's Tiptoe Staccato

French Play Tune

Let's tip-toe stac-ca-to o-ver the keys, Come, let's go

stac-ca-to light as the breeze. Now we play le-ga-to

is-n't it nice? Smooth-ly we glide; it's like skat-ing on ice.

Back we go stac-ca-to, Let's do it twice!

42

Jumping Rope

When the second note of a two-note slur has a staccato dot, the release-gesture on that note will be sharper and more abrupt.

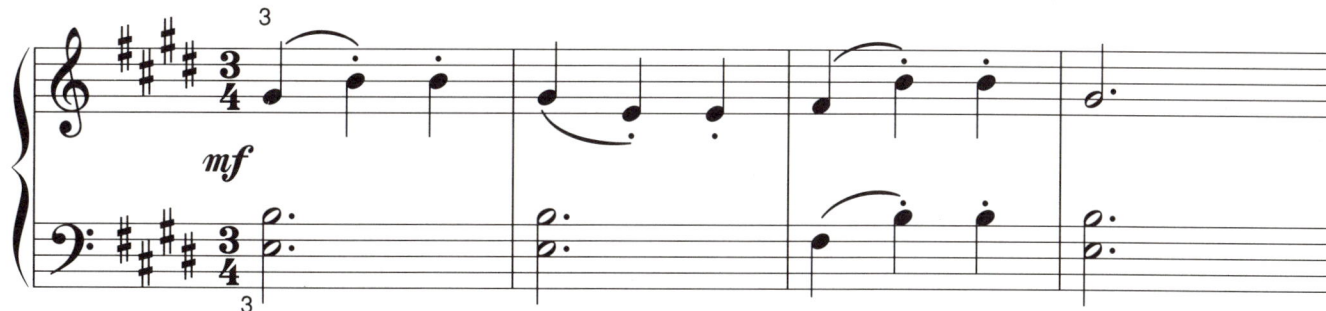

Autumn Song

Swedish Folk Tune

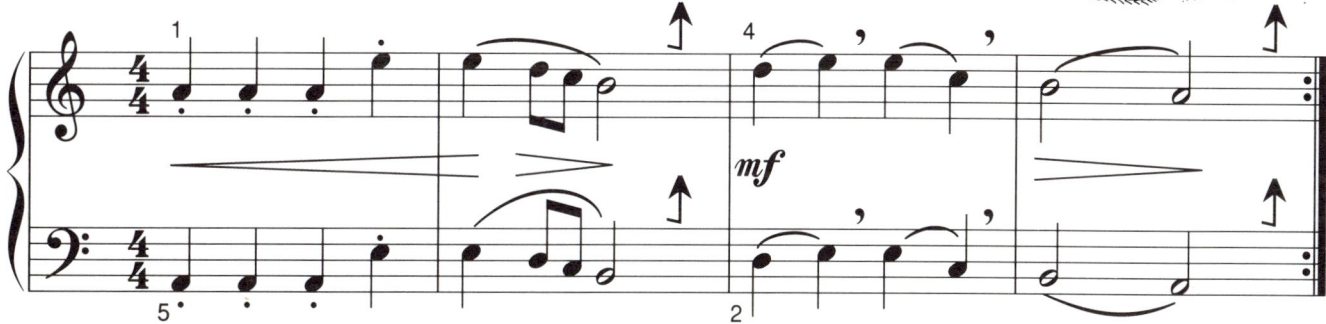

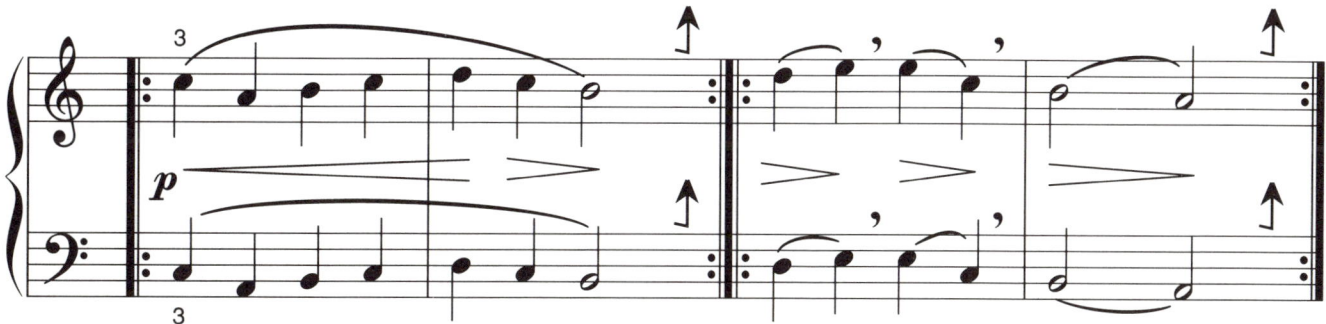

43

Double Notes (Harmonic Intervals)

Interval:	The **distance between two tones.***
Melodic Interval:	**Two notes played separately,** one after another, as in a melody. The interval between these two notes is called a *melodic interval.*
Harmonic Interval:	**Two notes sounded together** produce harmony. The interval between them is called a *harmonic interval.*

- Use good finger action, feeling the keys go down exactly together on the double notes.
- *Listen* to be sure that both notes sound exactly together.
- Play with separate hands; then play with hands together, if possible.

* See also Denes Agay's *Learning to Play Piano, Book 1*, page 43.

Ate Three Apples (and a Half)

Repeated thirds

D Major

- On the repeated thirds, fingers stay in contact with the keys, "riding them up."
- Play "Ate Three Apples" also in G and A positions.

Moderato

mf Ate three ap-ples | and a half, | Wish I did-n't do it; | Now I have a

tum-my-ache | Can you help me cure it? | Can you help me cure it?

Legato Thirds

- On the moving thirds, the hand, wrist and arm "floats" forward (release gesture).
- First, play hands separately. Then, play together, if possible.

mf (*p*)

mf (*p*)

* **Note to teacher**: If student is having difficulty playing this, have him or her first practice the outer voices separately, using fingers 3-4-5.

Little Serenade

Andante

Double-Note Frolic

Double-note staccato technic is the same as for single-note staccato. Make it feel the same in the hand, and have the same crisp, detached sound.

R.H.

L.H.

Allegretto scherzando

Drink to Me Only with Thine Eyes

Melody with accompanying double notes

G major:

- Bring out the melody with a rich, full tone, playing the accompanying double notes with somewhat less volume. Observe the separation mark (small release gesture) after the word "eyes." Slurs and phrases do not always end on the last note of a measure.
- The grouping of notes (phrasing) should always follow the natural, meaningful grouping of the words within the sentence.

Slowly

mp
p

Drink to me on - ly with thine eyes, And I will pledge with mine. Or leave a kiss with - in the cup, And I'll not ask for wine.

mf

rit.

Gaining Independence of Hands

In playing piano our two hands almost always play different parts. They may differ in

Patterns: melodic or rhythmic;

Dynamics: one hand playing melody, the other accompanying on a softer level;

Touches: one hand playing legato, the other staccato, etc.

Five Short Pieces

These short pieces are duets between the hands. First one hand plays, then the other answers; next, they blend together in a pleasing duet. (In the first three pieces, the hands are in contrary motion; in the last two, hands move in parallel motion.)

Touch: Large legato group (five or more notes) with release.

Playing the large legato groups with right hand and then left hand:

1. "Drop" on the first note of the pattern. (Feel that fingertip.)

2. Transfer that same tone quality to other notes with legato touch.

3. Release key (last note of the pattern) by moving hand, wrist, and arm forward, rolling onto fingernail.

D Major

IV

V

Follow Me

In "Follow Me," one hand imitates the other. This type of composition is called a *canon* (or *round*, if it is sung).

Andante

Fol - low me to school, Fol - low ev - 'ry rule.

I will lead the way, Then you won't go a - stray.

Catch Me if You Can

- First play hands separately, feeling large legato groupings.
- Feel *one* impulse (one combined gesture of hand/wrist/arm) for each group.
- *Listen* for good legato and even tone throughout each group.

E Minor

The Gondolier*

Slowly floating

mp Gon - do - lier, your boat is en - chant - ing.

Please, good sir, may I have a ride?

p
mf
Row me down the wa - ters of Ven - ice,

Down ca - nals, a - float on the tide.

* From Denes Agay's *Learning to Play Piano, Book 1*, page 58.

Balancing Melody and Accompaniment

When playing melodies with accompanying patterns, the *melody* should always be played somewhat *louder* than the accompaniment. Here are a few suggestions for varying dynamics.

To play softly:

- Bring your palm a little closer to the keyboard, with the wrist slightly lower than normal playing postion.
- Strike the key with the fleshier part of the fingertip (without losing the normal curve of the finger.)
- Use gentler, smaller finger action.

To get a fuller, richer tone:

- Apply some weight when striking the key. Play with a "heavy hand feeling."
- Keep all joints (knuckles, wrist, elbow, shoulder) free and loose.

Playing Hands Together
One *f* or *mf*, the other *p*

- Practice hands separately (keeping in mind the suggestions listed above) until the two parts go together easily.
- *Listen* for the dynamic balance between the two hands (accompaniment somewhat softer than the melody).
- Play the following exercises with these dynamic plans:

1. Both hands: *p*	3. Right hand.: *mf*, Left hand: *p*
2. Both hands: *mf*	4. Right hand: *p*, Left hand: *mf*

A Touch of Blue*

"Sing out" the right-hand melody.

Slowly

Oh, boo hoo! Think I have the flu.

It's a nice day, But I can't play, I'm so blue!

Show the contrast in moods in these two pieces with your touches and tone quality.

The Big Parade

Marching tempo

The band is march-ing through the park, Oh what a nois-y

prom-e-nade; Hear the flute, toot-toot, Hear the drum, bum-bum, Here comes the big pa-rade!

* From Denes Agay's *Learning to Play Piano, Book 1*, page 49.

52

Handkerchief Dance

A Major

Notice the dynamic differences between the two hands.

mf

p

p

mf

The Birch Tree

C Minor

- Play this piece as a boisterous Russian dance.
- The dynamic level in the two hands should be the same. The open-fifth double notes in the accompaniment should sound like drum beats, accentuated and at least as loud as the melody.
- Use firm fingertips and a supple wrist to play this dance.

Moderately with vigor

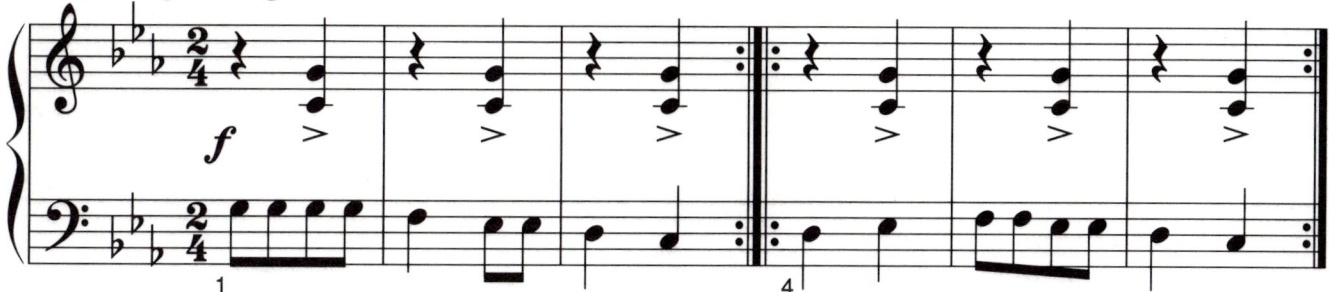

f

f

Legato and Staccato Together

Hands separately:

- Review legato touch, page 30.
- Review staccato touch, p. 32.

Hands together:

- Play slowly at first; then increase tempo.

No release is necessary after the three-note slurs.

54

Twins

Repeat the above exercise

1. Playing all quarter notes staccato
2. Playing left hand legato, right hand staccato
3. Playing left hand staccato, right hand legato
4. Right hand follows left hand

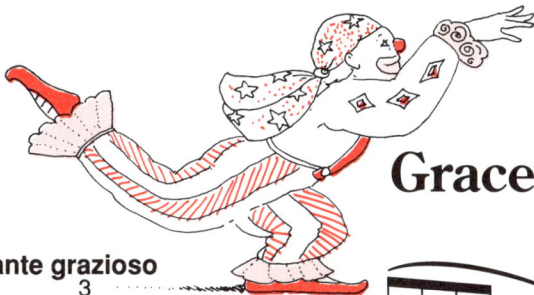

Graceful Clown

Andante grazioso

Sabbath Candles

This quiet, reverent piece is based on an "Oriental" five-finger pattern:

The repeated notes and small legato groups are played primarily with finger action; wrist and arm are quiet. No release is necessary after the left-hand two-note slurs.

Jewish Folk Melody

Slowly, tenderly

Some Folks Do

F Major

Touches:
- Repeated staccato notes with changing fingers
- Repeated staccato notes with same finger
- Larger legato groupings
- Balance of melody and accompaniment

Stephen Foster

F Minor

Variation on "Some Folks Do"

"Some Folks Do" may be repeated.

Little March

Melody in thirds

- Practice right-hand thirds with careful releases.
  (Review double note technic on page 44 and releases on page 39.)
- *Listen* for balance of melody and accompaniment.

A **triad** is **three notes** sounded together.	A **chord** is **three or more** notes sounded together.

Fanfares

- Play triads, solid or broken, with firm nail joints.
- After playing each solid chord, relax knuckle joints (while holding keys down), and then release.

Solemn Procession

- Feel fingers 1 and 5 play exactly together.
- Use a small release gesture (on third finger) after each two-note slur.
- After playing each half-note triad, relax and release forward toward knuckles.

A full, rich tone-quality will fit the mood of this piece.

Triads with White Keys Only

Play first with right hand, then with left hand one octave lower.

Solid Chords　　**Broken Chords**　　**Divided Chords**

C Major

F Major

G Major

A Minor

D Minor

E Minor

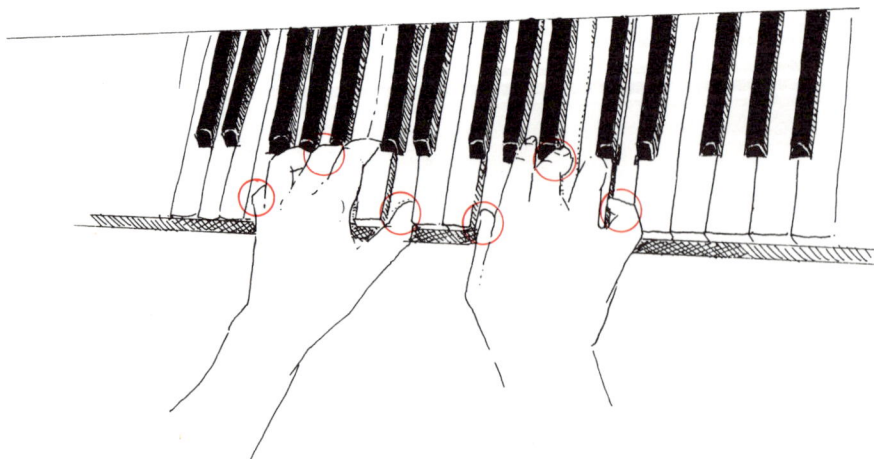

Triads with Third Finger on Black Key

Play first with right hand, then with left hand one octave lower.

Solid Chords   **Broken Chords**   **Divided Chords**

D Major

A Major

E Major

C Minor

F Minor

G Minor

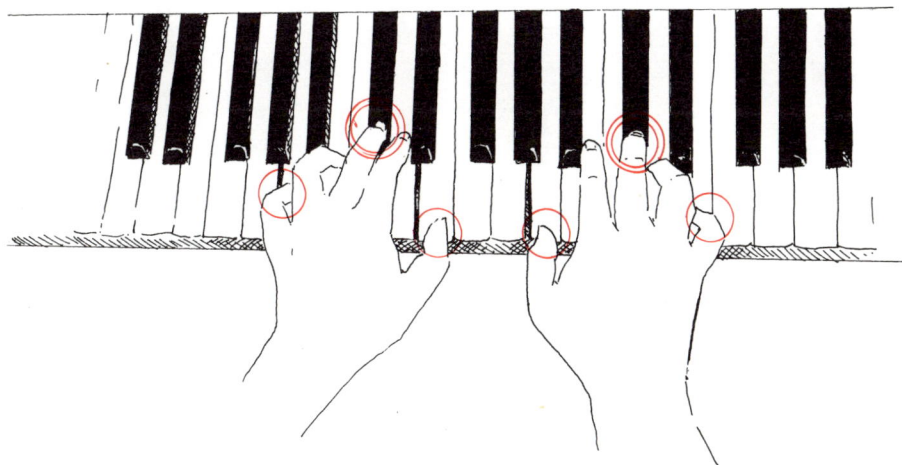

Gypsy Bagatelle

Melody with accompanying triads

'Round and 'Round We Go

The Organ Grinder's Waltz

Melody with accompanying divided chords

- Release after each four-measure legato phrase.
- Balance melody and accompanying chords.

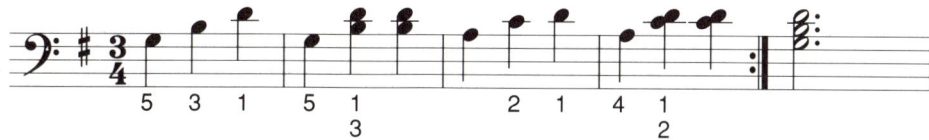

With a lilt

Triads and Slurs

- Shifting five-note patterns
- Staccato triads
- Two-note slurs
- Four-note slurs